A **TSR**™ GRAPHIC NOVEL

the

saga

B O O K • T H R E E

written by
Roy Thomas

illustrated by
Tony DeZuniga

lettered by
Jean Simek

colored by
Steve Oliff
and
Olyoptics

TSR, Inc.

Penguin Books

This graphic novel is adapted from
Book 1 of *Dragons of Winter Night*,
Volume 2 of the *DRAGONLANCE® Chronicles*,
by Margaret Weis and Tracy Hickman

Project Coordinator
JEFFREY BUTLER

Editorial Assistance
MARY KIRCHOFF   **JAMES M. WARD**

Production Assistance
PAUL HANCHETTE   **PEGGY COOPER**

Cover Illustration
JEFF EASLEY

Graphic Design
STEPHANIE TABAT

the
DragonLance
saɢa
B O O K • T H R E E
©Copyright 1988 TSR, Inc.
All Rights Reserved.

PENGUIN BOOKS

Published by the Penguin Group
27 Wrights Lane, London W8 5TZ, England
Viking Penguin Inc., 40 West 23rd Street, New
York, New York 10010 U.S.A.
Penguin Books Australia Ltd, Ringwood, Victo-
ria, Australia
Penguin Books Canada Ltd, 2801 John Street,
Markham, Ontario, Canada L3R 1B4
Penguin Books (NZ) Ltd, 182-190 Wairau Road,
Auckland 10, New Zealand

Penguin Books Ltd, Registered Offices: Har-
mondsworth, Middlesex, England

First Published in the USA by TSR, Inc. 1988.
Distributed to the book trade in the USA by
Random House, Inc. and in Canada by Random
House of Canada, Ltd.
Distributed to the toy and hobby trade by
regional distributors.
First published in Great Britain by Penguin
Books 1989 under license from TSR, Inc.
10 9 8 7 6 5 4 3 2 1

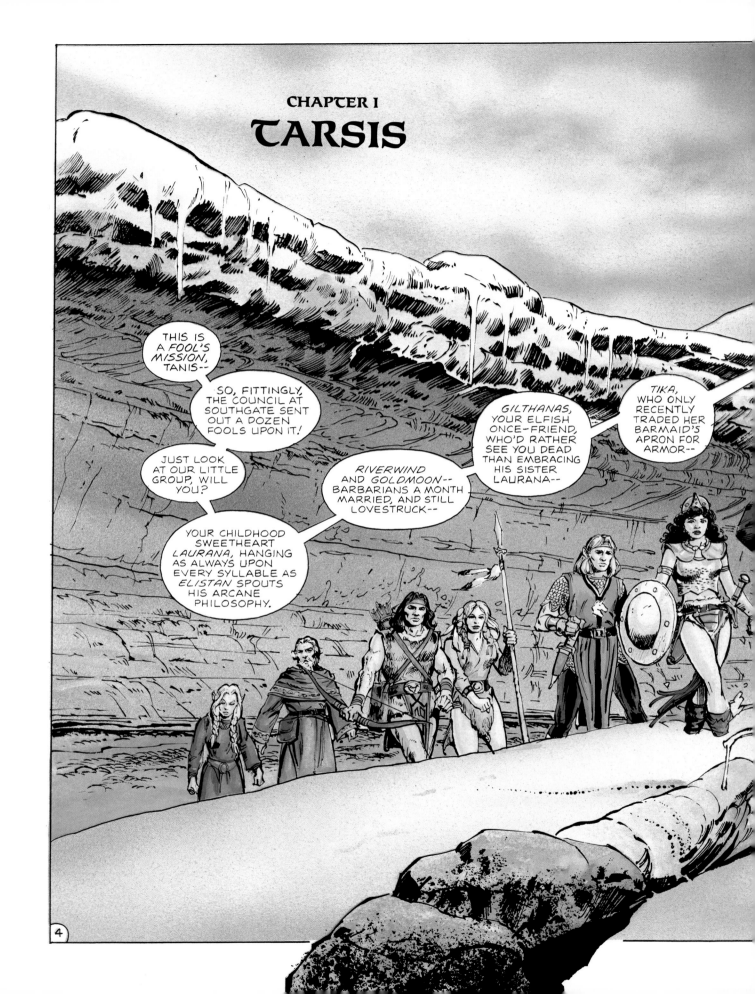

THE MAGICIAN MUST BE UP THERE.

LET THEM BE, PLEASE. WE WILL COME WITH YOU PEACEFULLY.

YOU HAVE MY WORD OF HONOR ON THAT.

VERY WELL. BUT TWO OF YOU GUARDS STAY HERE AT THE STAIR.

OTHERS WILL COVER THE REMAINING EXITS.

LAURANA...

FACE FORWARD!

QUIT SIGNALING TO YOUR FRIENDS UP THERE!

YOU'RE MISTAKEN, GUARD...

THERE'S NO ONE THERE.

14

UH-OH! THAT CROWD UP AHEAD LOOKS LIKE TROUBLE, TANIS!

IT'S BECAUSE OF *ME!* EVEN AFTER THREE CENTURIES, THEY REMEMBER THE SUPPOSED BETRAYAL OF TARSIS BY THE *SOLAMNIC KNIGHTS.*

PAY THEM NO MIND, STURM, AND THEY'LL NOT DARE BOTHER US.

DOG IN ARMOR!

WON'T THEY, HALF-ELF?

UNNGN--!

YOUR MOTHERS ALL WERE GULLY-DWARVES!

SHUT UP, TASSLEHOFF! YOU'RE JUST MAKING IT WORSE.

:MMFFF.!: WHO--?

WE'VE GOT THE KENDER!

OVER HERE, THEN--HURRY!

THE COUNCIL'S DOWN THIS WAY, STRANGERS.

YOU'RE LUCKY WE DON'T GUT YOU ALL, FOR INCITING A RIOT! *HA HA HA HA*

WHERE'S *TAS?* THAT MISERABLE KENDER GOT US *INTO* THIS, AND NOW HE--

HUSH, FLINT! I ONLY PRAY THE OTHERS SNEAK AWAY AS EASILY AS HE SEEMS TO HAVE!

15

WHERE CAN THEY HAVE BEEN TAKEN? IT HAS BEEN MORE THAN AN HOUR...

STURM WON'T LET ANYTHING HAPPEN TO THEM, NEVER FEAR.

I WISH YOU WOULD ALL RELAX.

MY SPELL KEEPS THE GUARDS DOWNSTAIRS, DOESN'T IT?

I COULD USE SOME QUIET, THAT I MAY STUDY A FEW MORE.

RAISTLIN, WOULD YOU TELL ME ABOUT... KITIARA?

YOU'VE NEVER MET... YET SHE IS YOUR RIVAL, EH?

IF NOT FOR MY ELDER HALF-SISTER KITIARA, I WOULD HAVE DIED IN CHILDBIRTH, AS OUR MOTHER DID.

AT FIFTEEN SHE LEFT HOME TO EARN HER LIVING BY THE SWORD.

AFTER SHE MET TANIS... SHE TRAVELED WITH THE REST OF US FROM TIME TO TIME.

AND WHY DO YOU ALL FOLLOW TANIS, WHEN HE IS A--

A BASTARD HALF-ELF?

THE OTHERS FOLLOW HIM BECAUSE HE LISTENS TO HIS FEELINGS... AND REALIZES THAT SOMETIMES A LEADER MUST THINK WITH HIS HEART AND NOT HIS HEAD.

REMEMBER THAT.

I NOTICE YOU LEAVE OUT YOURSELF.

IF YOU ARE AS INTELLIGENT AND POWERFUL AS YOU CLAIM, WHY DO YOU FOLLOW TANIS?

I DO NOT FOLLOW HIM, GIRL OF QUALINOST...

TANIS AND I SIMPLY HAPPEN TO BE TRAVELING IN THE SAME DIRECTION...

...AT LEAST FOR THE MOMENT.

...YOU COULD DO ME ANOTHER FAVOR, BY GIVING ME YOUR ASSISTANCE.

STURM IS CLEARLY SMITTEN WITH ALTHANA STARBREEZE, TANIS.

AND NO GOOD CAN COME OF IT, FOR THE SILVANESTI ARE A PROUD AND HAUGHTY RACE, EVEN FOR US ELVES.

FEARING THE LOSS OF THEIR WAY OF LIFE, THEY REFUSE TO HAVE EVEN THE SLIGHTEST CONTACT WITH HUMANS.

OVER SUCH MATTERS WERE THE KINSLAYER WARS FOUGHT, HUNDREDS OF YEARS AGO!

I KNOW, GILTHANAS, I KNOW.

THIS IS ALL WE NEEDED!

AT LEAST THEY'RE MARCHING US TO JAIL BY THE BACK WAY, TO AVOID ANOTHER RIOT.

WE CAN MAKE A BID FOR FREEDOM-- IF WE CAN GET STURM'S ATTENTION OFF THE PRINCESS FOR A MOMENT.

FLINT STANDS READY, ANYWAY, AND STURM WILL--

HALT!

UH-OH.

NOW WHAT?

20

32

HELLO ABOVE! WE'RE TRA--*MMMFF!*

CRY OUT, TIKA, AND YOU ADD *DRACONIANS* AND *GOBLINS* TO TANIS'S LIST.

AYE. THEY'RE THE ONLY CREATURES UP THERE LIABLE TO HEAR US THROUGH ALL THAT RUBBLE.

STILL, WE MUST-- *EH?*

LISTEN! I HEAR VOICES...

...A *WASTE OF TIME*, I TELL YOU.

AYE! THERE'S NO ONE ALIVE IN THIS MESS!

GOBLINS...

KEEP DIGGING, YOU MISERABLE DOG-EATERS-- OR WHEN I COME BACK YOU'LL ANSWER TO ME!

AND AT LEAST ONE *DRACONIAN*... ->KOFF!<-

IF ONLY I WEREN'T-- ->KOF<- ->KOF<- -- TOO TIRED TO CONCENTRATE-- ON ANOTHER SPELL...

WHAT'RE WE LOOKING FOR IN THIS RUBBLE, ANYWAY? SILVER? JEWELS?

NAW. *SPIES*, OR SOME SUCH-- WANTED PERSONALLY BY THE *DRAGON HIGHLORD*, THE WAY I HEAR IT.

TH-THEIR VOICES ARE GETTING LOUDER...,

BECAUSE THEY ARE GETTING *NEARER*.

WAIT! *NEW* SOUNDS...

WHAT'S THAT?

LOOK OUT! THEY'RE-- AAAAAA

36

"LATER, DURING THE *AGE OF MIGHT*, THE KINGPRIEST OF ISTAR AND HIS CLERICS BECAME JEALOUS OF THE MAGIC-USERS' POWERS.

"IT WAS A SIMPLE MATTER FOR THEM TO STIR UP THE *PEOPLE* AGAINST THE WIZARDS.

"AND, STRONG AS WIZARDS ARE, THEY MUST *SLEEP* FROM TIME TO TIME...AND ARE THUS VULNERABLE.

"THE TOWERS OF HIGH SORCERY, WHERE WE MAGICIANS MUST PASS OUR FINAL, GRUELING TESTS, WERE THE NATURAL TARGETS OF THE FEAR-MADDENED MOBS.

"TWO OF THE THREE DRAGON ORBS WERE DESTROYED WHEN THEIR TOWERS FELL.

"AND KNOWLEDGE OF THE OTHER THREE ORBS PERISHED WHEN ALL SURVIVING WIZARDS TRAVELED TO THE ONE TOWER WHICH WAS NEVER THREATENED;

"THE *TOWER OF WAYRETH* IN THE KHAROLIS MOUNTAINS.

MY HERB-TRANCE...TELLS ME LITTLE MORE...

...SAVE THAT IT WAS SAID *GREAT EVIL* WOULD COME TO THOSE NOT STRONG IN MAGIC, WHO TRIED TO COMMAND THE ORBS.

"STRONG IN MAGIC"? MY *FATHER*--!

HE STAYED BEHIND WITH THE ORB, ALHANA.

COULD IT HAVE BEEN-- TO USE IT?

I...I DO NOT KNOW...

L-LEAVE ME ALONE...!

Chapter IV

SILVANESTI

BEFORE WE REACH SILVANESTI, HALF-ELF, I SHOULD TELL YOU HOW MY FATHER, *LORAC,* ACQUIRED A *DRAGON-ORB.*

YEARS AGO, HE SURVIVED AND PASSED *THE TEST* AT THE TOWER OF HIGH SORCERY AT *ISTAR,* WHERE THIS ONE WAS KEPT.

DURING THE ORDEAL, HE SAYS THE ORB *SPOKE* TO HIM, OR AT LEAST TO HIS MIND, SAYING-- *"IF YOU LEAVE ME HERE, I WILL PERISH AND THE WORLD WILL BE LOST!"*

THUS, FAR FROM STEALING THE ORB, HE SAW HIMSELF AS *RESCUING* IT...THOUGH WHAT ELSE HE MIGHT KNOW OF IT, I COULD NOT--

EH?

WHAT IS IT, ALHANA?

WHY ARE WE DESCENDING WHILE WE'RE STILL SOME DISTANCE FROM THE CITY?

THEN WE WALK! IT CANNOT BE FAR OR HARD TO FIND, EVEN AT DUSK.

NO, CARAMON. BUT THE GRIFFONS OF THE SILVENESTI ELVES ARE AMONG THE MOST *LOYAL* OF THE GODS' CREATURES.

THESE, REMEMBER, FLEW INTO TARSIS THROUGH SWARMS OF *DRAGONS* WITHOUT APPARENT FEAR...

I DO NOT KNOW! OF A SUDDEN, THE GRIFFONS REFUSE TO OBEY MY COMMANDS!

THEY WON'T TELL ME WHY-- ONLY THAT WE MUST TRAVEL ON OUR OWN FROM HERE.

...SO WHAT ARE THEY AFRAID OF IN *SILVANESTI?*

43

CARAMON--!

MISHAKAL! HELP ME, GODDESS, TO HELP MY FRIEND!

M-MY THANKS, GOLDMOON. ALREADY... I FEEL...

YOU!

WH-WHO IS IT, RAIST?

TO WHOM DO YOU SPEAK?

I NEED YOUR HELP... NOW, AS BEFORE.

OUR BARGAIN REMAINS.

WHAT? YOU ASK FOR MORE?

NAME IT, THEN!

... I ACCEPT.

48

--BUT--DID RAISTLIN--GOT HERE FIR--

UNNNH

NO...

THUK!

STURM? WAS IT YOU WHO--?

KITIARA!?

I HEARD YOU NEEDED SOME HELP, TANIS.

SEEMS I WAS RIGHT.

HELLO, KITIARA. SO YOU'RE HERE, TOO.

STURM? WONDERFUL! JUST LIKE OLD TIMES!

SHALL WE ENTER THE TOWER...ALL TOGETHER?

WE...MIGHT AS WELL...

53

GOLDMOON!

WHERE ARE YOU, MY BELOVED?

I'LL FIGHT MY WAY BACK TO YOU--

-- IF IT MUST BE THROUGH A *RIVER* OF SKULLFACED ELVES!

WHAT? WHO'S THERE?

QUE-SHU! MY TRIBESMEN! IT IS I-- RIVERWIND!

YOU BROUGHT THE *BLUE CRYSTAL STAFF* AMONG US!

THE DESTRUCTION OF OUR VILLAGE WAS YOUR FAULT! YOUR FAULT!

BUT-- I DID NOT MEAN TO! I--

PLUNK

F-FORGIVE MEEEEEE!

54

I AM... DREAMING!

NONE OF THIS IS REAL...

...NOTHING BUT THE RING I CLENCH...SO PAINFULLY IN MY HAND!

YES! PAIN! I FEEL PAIN... REAL PAIN...

THE RING IS REAL--

--AND NOTHING ELSE!

WHAT? THE RING--

IT'S GONE!

AS IS--\>KOF!\< \>KOFF!\< -- THE DRAGON, TANIS.

OR HAD YOU NOT NOTICED?

THE ORB SENT THE DRAGON AWAY...\>KOFF!\< WHEN IT REALIZED IT COULD NOT DEFEAT ME...\>KOFF!\<...AS I WAS.

A CH-CHILD COULD \>KOFFF!\<... DEFEAT ME NOW!

THE OTHERS ARE GONE, AS WELL--LAURANA... KITIANA..., STURM. ARE THEY-- AND CARAMON--?

I... DO NOT KNOW. YOU LIVED, HALF-ELF, BECAUSE YOUR LOVE WAS STRONG. I LIVED... BECAUSE OF MY AMBITION.

WE CLUNG TO SUCH REALITIES... IN THE MIDST OF THE TERROR. WHO CAN TRULY SAY--\>KOF!\<--WITH THE OTHERS?

I CAN, RAIST.

CARAMON!

I AM TIRED, CARAMON...

AND THERE IS STILL MUCH TO BE DONE... BEFORE THIS NIGHTMARE IS TRULY ENDED.

I NEED... YOUR HELP, BROTHER.

AND I AM HERE.

65

THE ORB CALLED *CYAN BLOOD-BANE* HERE TO GUARD THE CITY...

...AND THE DRAGON DECIDED TO DESTROY IT INSTEAD, BY WHISPERING NIGHTMARES INTO LORAC'S EAR.

THE ELFKING'S BELIEF IN THE NIGHTMARE WAS SO STRONG--HIS EMPATHY WITH HIS LAND SO GREAT--

--THAT THE NIGHTMARE BECAME *REALITY.*

YOU *KNEW* WE FACED THIS!

YOU KNEW--THE MOMENT WE WERE SET DOWN BY THE GRIFFONS!

PERHAPS. PERHAPS NOT.

I NEED NOT REVEAL MY KNOWLEDGE OR ITS SOURCE TO YOU.

YOU *WILL* REVEAL IT, OR BY THE GODS, I'LL--

OHHHHH...

WHO'S THAT?

IT'S *ALHANA STARBREEZE!*

SHE CROUCHES BESIDE HER FATHER'S THRONE, SO UNMOVING WE DID NOT HEAR HER TILL SHE MOANED.

ALHANA...?

TANIS HALF-ELVEN? I...DID NOT HEAR YOU ENTER.

HOW DID YOU GET HERE? WHAT HAPPENED?

THE DRAGON CAPTURED ME...BROUGHT ME HERE, HOPING TO MAKE MY FATHER MURDER ME.

BUT NOT EVEN IN HIS NIGHTMARE COULD LORAC HARM HIS OWN CHILD.

SO CYAN TORTURED HIM WITH VISIONS-- OF WHAT HE WOULD DO TO ME.

MY POOR FATHER...

67

RAISTLIN... YOU SAID THE ORB SUMMONED THE DRAGON HERE, THEN SENT IT AWAY AGAIN.

IS THE ORB STILL IN CONTROL HERE?

ALLOW ME, MILADY.

AN INTERESTING QUESTION.

LET US SEE, SHALL WE?

ARAHK-TLOTAC LIPOCHTA...

...ZALCOATL HUITLA.

RAISTLIN-- WHAT--?

DO NOT FEAR. THE CRIMSON AURA WAS MY SPELL.

THE GLOBE IS STILL IN CONTROL.

OF LORAC?

OF ITSELF. IT HAS RELEASED LORAC... BECAUSE IT CAN NO LONGER USE HIM.

WE CAN FREE THE ELFKING NOW.

HE LIVES... FOR THE TIME BEING... BUT HIS LIFEBEAT IS WEAK.

CAN THE ORB STILL BE OF USE TO US?

YES.

IF WE DARE.

WAIT! LORAC IS--

FATHER--!

SLEEP, FATHER. THE NIGHTMARE IS ENDED...THE DRAGON GONE.

...ALHANA... ALIVE...?

BUT I... I SAW YOU DIE, DAUGHTER!

I SAW YOU DIE A HUNDRED TIMES. HE WANTED *ME* TO KILL YOU, BUT I WOULD NOT.

THOUGH I KNOW NOT WHY... AS I HAVE KILLED SO MANY.

PLEASE, FATHER...

YOU MUST REST NOW. THE NIGHTMARE IS OVER.

SILVANESTI IS SAFE.

IS IT, RAISTLIN?

TRUE, I SEE NO *UNDEAD ELF-WARRIORS* STALKING THE WOODS BELOW...

...BUT THE MISSHAPEN TREES LORAC CREATED BY HIS DREAM STILL ENDURE OUTSIDE.

69

WILL OUR PEOPLE RETURN, ALHANA?

OF COURSE.

A LIE, MY CHILD? SINCE WHEN HAVE THE ELVES LIED TO EACH OTHER?

I THINK PERHAPS WE HAVE ALWAYS LIED TO OURSELVES, FATHER.

GOLDMOON, THE CLERIC OF MISHAKAL THE HEALER, SAYS THE ANCIENT GODS DID NOT ABANDON KRYNN.

THEY BUT WAIT FOR MEN-- AND ELVES FIND THEM AGAIN.

THEN I GIVE MYSELF TO THE LAND.

BURY MY BODY IN THE SOIL, DAUGHTER.

IT SHALL BE DONE...

...F-FATHER.

AS MY LIFE... BROUGHT THIS CURSE...UPON THE LAND...

...SO PERHAPS... MY DEATH WILL BRING...

...ITS... BLESSINNNN✂

71

...NOW THAT WE HAVE RESTED ALL DAY, MY FRIENDS, WE MUST DEPART SILVANESTI.

I SHALL CARRY THE ORB.

ISN'T IT RATHER TOO LARGE FOR YOU, RAIST?

PERHAPS I CAN HELP...

MY FATHER ALWAYS CARRIED THE ORB IN THIS SACK.

HE SAID IT WAS GIVEN HIM IN THE TOWER OF HIGH SORCERY...

THANK YOU, MY LADY.

YES, I THINK THIS SACK WILL DO VERY NICELY.

BUT-- IT'S SO SMALL...

JISTRAH TAGOPAR AST MOIRPARANN KINI.

NOW... HAND IT TO ME, CARAMON.

THE ORB, IT-- IT'S SHRINKING!

OF COURSE, MY DEAR BROTHER.

HOW ELSE COULD IT FIT IN SO TINY A SACK?

72

AND THEN AGAIN...

RAISTLIN... THINGS CAN NEVER AGAIN BE THE SAME BETWEEN US, CAN THEY?

NO. BUT SUCH WAS >KOF! KOFF!<---THE PRICE I PAID.

...PERHAPS IT IS WE WHO HAVE GROWN, EH?

PRICE?

TO WHOM?

FOR WHAT, MAGE?

DO NOT QUESTION, HALF-ELF. I CANNOT TELL YOU THE ANSWER... >KOFF! KOFF!<

...BECAUSE I DO NOT KNOW IT MYSELF.

...THE GRIFFONS WILL COME NOW THAT THE EVIL IS GONE, ALHANA, AND BEAR YOU TO YOUR PEOPLE IN ERGOTH.

YES, TANIS. WE WILL DO WHAT WE CAN TO HELP DEFEAT THE DRAGONS... AND ONLY THEN SHALL WE COME HOME TO RESTORE OUR TORTURED LAND.

AND WILL YOU FIND TIME TO GO TO SANCRIST? THE SOLAMNIC KNIGHTS THERE WOULD BE HONORED BY YOUR PRESENCE... PARTICULARLY ONE OF THEM.

COULD HE BE HAPPY HERE IN SILVANESTI, TANIS?

AND COULD I BE HAPPY, KNOWING THAT I MUST WATCH HIM AGE AND DIE-- WHILE I AM STILL IN MY YOUTH?

IF WE DENY LOVE BECAUSE WE FEAR THE PAIN OF LOSS, MY LADY...

...THEN OUR LIVES WILL BE EMPTY, OUR LOSS THE GREATER.

73

FIN

Our adventurers return in
The DRAGONLANCE® Saga, Book Four.